Lonny

the Long Armed Puppeteer

A Day to Remember

DREW NOWLIN

authorHOUSE

AuthorHouse™
1663 Liberty Drive
Bloomington, IN 47403
www.authorhouse.com
Phone: 1 (800) 839-8640

Published by AuthorHouse 01/05/2016

ISBN: 978-1-5049-6939-0 (sc)
ISBN: 978-1-5049-6940-6 (e)

Walk behind Lonny and then you will see

His arms can stretch to the top of a tree.

He's just as lazy as a boy can be

Making puppets all day, humming with glee.

'Yep, my classmates made up that poem about me. My name is Lonny and I am just a normal kid. Oh, but I can make my arms stretch to great lengths. Sometimes it comes in handy. Sometimes it's a little annoying. But it always helps me do what I've always wanted to do … perform with puppets. And this is a story about me.'

Lonny McMurray

In a simple town, with simple people, who had simple values there lived a simple family with a not so simple little boy. The McMurray family lived in the next to last house on Sunset Avenue and enjoyed a humble life. The father worked in construction and was away quite a lot, but he still came home every night to be with his family. The mother created websites for environmental issues and always retained a firm belief in fighting for what was right. Krissy, their younger child was a sweet girl fascinated with cute stuffed animals and gory zombie films. And then there was Lawrence, but since he hated that name everyone called him Lonny. He was the oldest child and Lonny didn't really like anything, but he was well known in the town because he had one miraculous trait. Lonny could stretch his arms to massive lengths whenever he wanted to.

Lonny had this ability ever since he was born. Over the years the other kids laughed and ridiculed him, so Lonny learned early on that some people could be cruel, and those were the ones he didn't need to be around. Bullies in the school would tie him to the flagpole like a pretzel or the snobby girls would make him use his arms for double dutch, so Lonny tended to be alone and didn't talk to most people. And as the treatment worsened over the years, he preferred not to show people what he could do in public. Lonny mainly used his stretchiness in his home or in privacy.

Spending a lot of time with no one to talk to Lonny started to read books about different crafts and skills from around the world and, if it was interesting enough, he'd try them. He tried basket weaving for a while, but the baskets never managed to stay together. Lonny took up bird watching, but always managed to scare the birds. At one point Lonny wanted to learn to play the cello, but it became a bit too cumbersome. However, one day after reading a very entertaining article, Lonny started to make puppets to amuse himself and found he had a knack

for it. Having the ability to extend his arms came in quite handy for this and Lonny decided this is what he wanted to do. His parents did not object to him being a puppeteer, but really didn't encourage him either. Krissy, on the other hand, was the only person who Lonny really felt supported him even though they still had their huge disagreements.

School had just gotten back in and Lonny was in 4th grade. Lonny was 9 years old and usually pondered what 10 would be like. He was walking to school, just looking around at the trees, the sky, the dead bugs on the pavement, and the news helicopter circling the morning traffic jams. The day was quite nice and a slight breeze kept it from being too hot. Krissy was a few steps behind him trying to keep up. Krissy was keen on telling everyone she was 27 and ½ months younger than her brother and she greatly enjoyed being so. This morning however, Krissy was much more talkative than normal.

'Hey Lonny, I'm worried about Keith, a boy in my class who lives on our street,' Krissy began. Lonny did not answer. 'He has been really flahplah.' Krissy loved to make up words that had meaning to her, but Lonny didn't mind.

'What does flahplah mean?' Lonny asked still walking towards school.

'Don't you know anything? When someone is flahplah their eyes are all puffy, and they don't have any energy at P.E., and they keep falling out of their chair in class. You know … flahplah!' She exclaimed.

'Sounds to me like he is just a little tired and needs to sleep,' Lonny suggested.

'Maybe.' Krissy admitted. 'Maybe I could invite him to watch a zombie movie marathon with me. That might help him drift off to sleep.'

'Some kids don't find brain eating monsters as relaxing as you do, Kris,' Lonny said.

'You just can't see the deeper meaning,' Krissy scoffed.

'Probably not,' Lonny said in an attempt to end the conversation. He wondered how his cute little sister, who insists on taking an adorable

 stuffed monkey to school, could possibly not be traumatized by walking corpses attempting to eat the living. Fortunately for

him, Divya was walking to school that day too. She was Krissy's best friend and she called out to them as she cautiously ran across the street to join Krissy. Lonny knew what was about to ensue, so before Divya had even reached the curb Lonny put his headphones on and began listening to his music. Only a couple more blocks to go and then another day would begin.

The classroom was, as normal, rowdy and anxious to get out for play period by early afternoon. Lonny's class had the good fortune of having lunch and then a very short lesson before being excused to play. The day, up to that point, had been rather uneventful as they muddled through a math lesson. Lonny did all of his work sitting in the middle row, furthest from the classroom door and closest to the

windows. He preferred to remain as unnoticed as possible. His peers in the back were always getting reprimanded due to their lack of focus, while the kids up front were a little too eager to please the teacher with their cheerful wit. Lonny preferred to peer outside, especially on beautiful clear days like that day, when the windows were open.

Lonny was not a poor student, just a dreamer. If called upon by the teacher, Ms. Feingold, he would usually get the answer right and then drift back off to looking out the window. Lonny liked Ms. Feingold as a teacher. She wasn't too strict and never treated any of his classmates as inferiors or babies, so he was happy to do the work and listen when he needed to.

'Alright class, does anyone have any questions about this?' Ms. Feingold asked, referring to a math equation on the board.

'No Ms. Feingold,' the entire class said at once. Ms. Feingold insisted that if she asked a question to the class, the entire class would respond.

'Then I think we have just enough time for one more math problem,' Ms. Feingold admitted as she turned back to the chalkboard and began writing.

The class huffed and puffed, all except Lonny. Nothing really bothered Lonny about Ms. Feingold, except that she always wore something that was plaid. While Lonny imagined the overall amount of plaid that must be in her closet, suddenly an all too familiar feeling of a paper football hit the back of his head. Three of the boys in the back row had tormented Lonny since his kindergarten days.

The alpha of these three and the perpetrator of the paper football kick was a rude boy named Alex Brimley.

Alex Brimley's timing was impeccable. He waited until Ms. Feingold's back was turned and he'd had plenty of practice so his aim was perfect. His two cronies, Jeff and Court, snickered under their breathe. They weren't the smartest kids in class, but they were the most intimidating. Lonny was amazed that between the three of them they couldn't recite the pledge of allegiance, so Lonny chose to ignore them in hopes they would occupy themselves some other way for the next couple minutes.

'Hey noodle arms,' Alex whispered. 'Perhaps instead of playing with dolls, maybe you should work cleaning gutters. You'd never need a ladder, only the longest pair of rubber gloves ever made.'

Lonny didn't respond. As insults went that one was pretty tame, but nonetheless Alex and his pals were completely amused. He peered at the clock hoping time would speed up. Normally when the class breaks for a free period, Lonny would stay under a tree and read some of his favorite books.

'Or better yet Looney,' Alex continued, making a mockery of Lonny's name. 'A better job would be a human toilet plunger. You can come over to my house later, cause I know after a few burritos I'll need your help.'

It was finally the top of the hour and it was time for a break. All the hustle and bustle started as kids raced to line up at the door. Lonny was fetching a book out of his desk when Court took it from him and threw it out the window.

'I heard of a book drive, but never a book fly,' Jeff said.

The three thugs laughed and laughed on the way out. Lonny didn't know what to do. He was tired of them always picking on him. He sat at his desk and looked out the window in an empty room. Ms. Feingold didn't notice Lonny at first, as she sat at her desk, but when she saw him with a perplexed look on his face she walked over to him.

'What's wrong?' She asked.

'Day in and day out Alex and his friends pick on me. I'm sick of it but I don't know what to do.'

'Lonny you are a very bright boy with a remarkable gift,' Ms. Feingold responded.

'Look I don't want to talk about my arms....' Lonny started.

'I'm not talking about that.' She interrupted. 'I was simply saying you have a very kind heart. You try to stay on your own, but I've seen you when you thought no one was looking. You like helping people, don't you? You help your sister, your parents, ... even me, but I'm not sure if you know that it's alright to take a stand against those who would make fun of you for a minor difference.'

'Well ...' Lonny started.

'I know those boys are rotten to you, but you are just one of the many they pick on in my class.' Ms. Feingold confided. 'I would like nothing more than to suspend them for every terrible little thing they've done, but I can't see everything that they do. They're children, just like you, and they need to learn sooner or later that someone will take a stand.'

'But ...' Lonny started.

'You know, I think today they are going to play kick ball,' Ms. Feingold pondered. 'I always liked kick ball and I think it's a game you would be very good at. Don't you think?'

Lonny thought for a moment in silence and knew that his teacher was right about everything. This was the last straw. It was time to make a stand and take matters into his own hands and he had the perfect plan. Lonny stood up and scurried out of the room.

Lonny made his way outside and looked towards the field. The teams were being divided and, of course, the three morons were on the same team and weeding out the weaker kids for their opponents. Lonny was fed up with being made fun of and this was the perfect opportunity to get back at them.

Lonny walked up and immediately joined the opposing team.

'I'll pitch,' Lonny firmly stated. The other team laughed hysterically. Lonny had never shown any interest in playing any sports.

'Oh this is gonna be a piece of cake.' Alex boasted. 'Well short stuff, take the loser squad and try not to cry too much when we mop the floor with you.'

'We'll see,' Lonny said peering at Alex with fierce determination in his eyes. Lonny and his teammates walked out to the field and he huddled them together. 'Don't worry, we're gonna win this game. You all just worry about kicking and I'll take care of the rest.'

Lonny stood on the pitchers mound. No one had really seen him use his talents, especially not in sports, but now was a time for action. Lonny took the ball and rolled it towards the plate. The first kicker landed a solid blow and it went towards third base. Gwen, a little pigtailed girl, was on third and it was coming at her fast. She cringed away from the speeding orb, but then it was caught. Just like that, Lonny had extended his arms and caught the ball. His arms retracted back to him as Lonny called, 'You're out.'

Two more kickers tried, but Lonny was too good. Now his team was up to kick. He didn't have the strongest kickers on his team, but Lonny had a plan. He was the first one up as Alex took the mound to roll the ball. The first roll came right at Lonny and nowhere near home plate, so Lonny jumped out of the way.

'Sorry Looney,' Alex yelled. 'It's too bad your legs aren't made of rubber too, otherwise I might be worried.' Alex motioned for everyone to come closer with a confident grin on his face. Lonny always wondered why bullies always assumed that just because a person has a unique physical trait, in also means that they have a mental problem. Well Lonny was ready to show everyone that ever made fun of him he was just fine the way he was.

Alex rolled the ball, this time over the plate, and Lonny kicked it. It wasn't a great kick, but it sped towards third base. A young girl named Meghan picked up the ball quickly and hurled it to first. She was sure she'd gotten him out, since Lonny wasn't even running hard to get to base. Court was on first base and caught the ball as Lonny casually walked towards him.

'You're out, Loser,' Court screamed.

'Think again,' Lonny said as a smile creeped across his face. Court slowly looked down and saw that Lonny's hand was already on base. Lonny had simply extended his arm to get to base before Meghan  had even gotten the ball. 'I think that means I'm safe.'

Court cast a confused and angry glance at Lonny, then turned and threw the ball back to Alex.

'So what,' Alex scoffed. 'So you made it to first, it doesn't mean the rest of your crumby team can do that. You're still gonna lose.' Alex turned around and faced the next kicker, Chloe. Chloe was a very short, but bright young girl and really had no talent for kicking. Lonny could see that Chloe was scared and that Alex was going to roll a fast ball by the evil smile he had on his face.

'You only need to kick it lightly, Chloe,' Lonny yelled. All eyes turned to Lonny. 'It's Ok; I'll take care of the rest.'

'Shut up, Loser,' Alex demanded. He turned back to home plate and rolled a furious roll. Chloe stood there and kicked it as hard as she could. Alex had started to run after the ball as soon as he rolled it, so he could throw to second base. Chloe had just started to run from home plate when Alex had snagged the ball and turned to throw. However in that split second before he let the ball go, he saw Lonny's hand was already on second base. Alex clenched his teeth tight and was so fixated on Lonny he didn't even realize that Chloe had made it to first base. 'No Fair!' Alex yelled. 'You can't do that. Your feet have to touch the base, not your hands. Do it again and your team forfeits.'

'Ok,' Lonny said. 'I wanna be fair. You got it. My feet have to be on base, otherwise I'm out.'

Alex smugly walked back the pitcher's mound. All he could see was Lonny smirking back at him. He wasn't gonna try and throw to third base this time. Alex imagined Lonny actually running, making him an easy target for a swift kick ball right in the face. Alex resumed his place on the mound and didn't look at Lonny. Lonny gazed at Chloe, who was sweating under the hot sun, and silently reassured her it was ok. Tommy stepped to the plate. Alex loosed the ball again, only this time it was a lot slower, because he wanted it to get kicked. Alex hustled towards the plate like he'd done before and grabbed the kick ball. He turned with ball in hand, knowing full well that Lonny had no choice but to run and took aim at his target. Lonny was only a step off the base.

Alex had a crazed smile and said, 'Aww, the baby isn't even gonna try? Well here you go.' At that instant, Alex released a destructive throw right at Lonny. Staying cool and composed Lonny extended both arms at third base and grabbed it. Then to the astonishment of every person on that field, Lonny pulled himself feet first to the base and avoided the devastating impact of Alex's throw. The ball whizzed by Chloe and continued into the outfield. Alex's teammates scrambled to go get the ball.

'Run for home,' Lonny shouted. And the three had scored before the ball could even be recovered.

The entire game continued the same way. Lonny's team had dominated their opponents, who hadn't scored a single run, as they were drawing nearer to the end of the play period. Lonny was back on the mound and his entire team was rallying behind him. Alex was next to kick and he stomped to the plate. His whole team was irritated and embarrassed at their humiliating loss, but Alex was enraged.

'Still think we're a bunch of losers?' Lonny shouted from the mound.

'You little freak,' Alex bellowed. 'You will never get the best of me.'

Lonny was ready to roll the ball, but he'd allowed himself to be a bit too confident. The ball was released and headed right for home base. Alex ran at it and kicked the sphere with all his might, but he didn't want to kick it past Lonny. Instead Alex kicked it right at him.

Boom!!

Lonny was hit square in the face. As he left his feet everything became a blur and the entire world was silent. This feeling seemed to last for several minutes, until he landed on the ground. Lonny's face throbbed from the force of the impact as the sunlight seemed to get even more intense. From the flat of his back and unable to stand, Lonny looked up and saw Alex's outline. The rest of Alex's team followed and surrounded Lonny while he was lying on the ground.

'You are pathetic,' Alex stated as he bent over and loomed over Lonny. 'It doesn't matter that you won this game, in life you will never be anything more than a wimp with freaky arms.' Alex stood up and started laughing, but the others behind him didn't laugh with him. Instead the mass of shadows parted and all Lonny could make out a bit of plaid. Then a hand was placed on Alex's shoulder.

'That wasn't very sportsmanlike conduct,' Ms. Feingold said. 'I'm afraid that little stunt has earned you a month of afterschool detention.' The rest of the class was speechless as Lonny's team encircled him and helped him to his feet. 'Please go to the principal's office and wait for me there.' Alex trudged away with his head held low as Lonny regained his balance and dusted himself off. 'Does anyone else wish to go to detention? From what I saw today, it's obvious that stricter rules need to be adhered to. And anyone who doesn't like it can take it up with the Principal and your parent's. Is that understood?'

'Yes Ms. Feingold,' the entire class said.

'Now go back to the room and please gather your belongings,' Ms. Feingold instructed. 'The school buses will be here soon.' Upon that statement, the rest of the class rushed back towards the school's front door.

'Thanks Lonny,' Chloe said and she quickly walked after the other students.

'Are you alright, Lonny?' Ms. Feingold asked.

'Yes Ms. Feingold,' Lonny responded, making sure his nose wasn't bleeding. They both shared a moment of relief now that the game was over.

'Well done Mr. McMurray. Now go and get your stuff.' Ms. Feingold said with a hint of pride peeking though.

Lonny started running for the classroom, but after a few steps he stopped. He turned back around and asked, 'Were you watching the whole time Ms. Feingold?'

'I told you I'm very fond of kick ball,' Ms. Feingold admitted as she handed him the book that was cast out of the class window earlier. Lonny took the book, smiled, and continued to run for the classroom to gather his school materials.

******

Krissy was waiting for Lonny at the corner for their normal walk back home. He was running a little late since he was still a bit groggy from the kick ball game.

'What happened to your face?' Krissy insisted. 'You've got a big bruise.'

'Nothing,' Lonny said as he started to lead her home. 'I just got hit in the face while we were playing kick ball.'

Krissy looked her brother over from head to toe. 'Something's different about you,' she commented.

'Really,' Lonny stated in astonishment. 'I've never felt better. Oh, by the way what was your friend's name that was feeling .... floopy?'

'It's flahplah,' Krissy corrected. 'Can't you understand proper English? Anyway his name is Keith.'

'You said he lives on our street, right?' Lonny continued.

'Yeah,' Krissy wondered.

'Well let's stop by his house on the way home and check on him,' Lonny suggested.

'That sounds great. I really think he needs someone to talk to,' Krissy exclaimed. The siblings raced to Keith's house, with Krissy well in the lead, and he was sitting on his front porch. His head was hanging low and he didn't notice the two approaching until they were a few steps away. 'Keith,' Krissy yelled. Keith raised his head and he had dark circles under his eyes. 'Why weren't you in school today?' Krissy asked.

'I'm not feeling too good,' Keith said with strain in his voice. 'I haven't been sleeping very well.'

'Why?' Lonny asked.

Keith looked at Lonny in utter shock that he was talking to him. 'This is my brother Lonny,' Krissy said. 'We just wanted to see if we could do anything  for you. So why can't you sleep?'

'It's embarrassing,' Keith confided.

'It's alright,' Krissy said sitting next to him. Lonny was always amazed that Krissy could be very compassionated when she wanted to be. 'What's wrong?'

'Well I've been having a lot of nightmares lately and I keep seeing monsters in my closet,' Keith said.

Lonny and Krissy both knew that monsters didn't really exist, but Lonny came up with a plan quickly. 'We'll come back tomorrow after school and I will bring something I think can help,' Lonny stated. Krissy looked up at him in curiosity, but knew her brother wouldn't say something like that unless he really meant it.

The next day after school Lonny and Krissy came up the road hauling a huge puppet. Keith let them into his room and they set up what appeared to be a giant monster puppet facing the closet.

'Now Keith, here's the plan,' Lonny explained. 'This is a scary monster puppet I made a while back, but I don't need anymore. Is it scary to you?' Keith slowly nodded his head. 'Good, that's the point. See us three know that it's just a puppet, made out of fabric, foam, and paint.' Keith nodded his head again. 'So there's no point in being scared of it,' Lonny continued.

'But what am I suppose to do with it?' Keith asked.

'Well we know it's fake, but the monsters in your closet don't,' Lonny added. 'So whenever you feel scared just climb in here.' Lonny opened a flap that led underneath the puppet's frame where a small pillow and blanket were located. 'You can stay in here and this fellow will scare all the other monsters away, no problem.'

'Really,' Keith said as he thought about it. 'Wow, that's really cool. I'll try it. Thanks you two.'

Krissy and Lonny left Keith's house feeling very proud of themselves. Lonny knew that as long as he used his talents to help others, it would make

him feel like he

belonged.

'Alright don't get all choked up about it. I just helped out a complete stranger with a little problem at the behest of my sister. It doesn't mean that everything will always be happily ever after. I'm still in school and there are plenty of days for new problems to surface, but after today I felt a rekindled sense of achievement for helping the outcasts. There is always someone that needs help and, if I can, maybe I can do something about it. If you really want to know about my next breakthrough then just read a little more about me, my family, and my stretchy arms. I think I'll take it easy this weekend and try to grab the traffic-copter as it flies over and heads for the big pool on the other side of town.'

Lonny McMurray

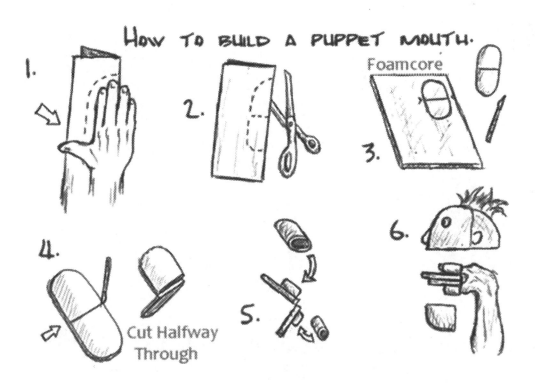

How To Build A Puppet Mouth.

1.

2.

Foamcore

3.

4.

Cut Halfway Through

5.

6.